VOICES OF THE FUTURE

STORIES FROM AROUND THE WORLD

Foreword by Irina Bokova,
Director General of UNESCO

With the support of
UNESCO

United Nations
Educational, Scientific and
Cultural Organization

Voices of Future Generations Children's Book Series

BLOOMSBURY EDUCATION
Bloomsbury Publishing Plc
50 Bedford Square, London, WC1B 3DP, UK

BLOOMSBURY, BLOOMSBURY EDUCATION and the Diana logo
are trademarks of Bloomsbury Publishing Plc

First published in Great Britain 2018
Text copyright © individual authors, 2018
Illustrations copyright © Marco Guadalupi, Giovana Medeiros,
Mona Meslier Menaua and Jhonny Nunez 2018

Kehkashan Basu, Diwa Boateng, Jona David, Anna Kuo, Allison Hazel Lievano-Gomez,
Lautaro Real, Tyronah Sioni, and Lupe Va'ai have asserted their rights under the
Copyright, Designs and Patents Act, 1988, to be identified as Authors of this work

A catalogue record for this book is available from the British Library

ISBN: HB: 978 1 4729 4943 1; ePub: 978 1 4729 4945 5; ePDF: 978 1 4729 4944 8

2 4 6 8 10 9 7 5 3 1

Cover and text design by Becky Chilcott

Printed and bound in India by Replika Press Pvt. Ltd.

All papers used by Bloomsbury Publishing Plc are natural, recyclable products
from wood grown in well managed forests. The manufacturing processes
conform to the environmental regulations of the country of origin

To find out more about our authors and books visit
www.bloomsbury.com and sign up for our newsletters

VOICES OF THE FUTURE

STORIES FROM AROUND THE WORLD

Foreword by Irina Bokova, Director General of UNESCO

BLOOMSBURY EDUCATION

LONDON OXFORD NEW YORK NEW DELHI SYDNEY

Contents

Foreword

This book provides a glimpse into the ways in which future generations conceive of − and have the ability to use − their voices for positivity and growth. It allows readers to understand the boundless possibilities for children to influence their communities and how children can view themselves as agents of growth.

In each story, *Voices of the Future* stresses the importance of creativity for children and lets them know how vital their imaginings can be for their families, communities, and the world in which they live. These stories invite readers into the imaginings of other children to let them understand how others see the world. At the same time, they open readers' minds to new possibilities and give them a platform for their own creative endeavours. Each story notes the importance of teamwork in identifying problems and working to overcome them.

It draws the reader into worlds that are better for everyone because people have handled problems together and have used their collective creativity to create new solutions.

Voices of the Future highlights the value of education as an essential vehicle for addressing real-world problems such as sustainable development, violence against women, discrimination against those with disabilities, intolerance, and

environmental destruction. It allows readers to view education as the basis on which to build a strong and vibrant society that can celebrate differences and share in accomplishments. The stories remind readers that education is a life-long process and that it does not end with each school day.

And *Voices of the Future* stresses the importance of listening to future generations in order to benefit the current and future world. From creating life-altering inventions to rebuilding communities and eco-systems, the children in each story demonstrate that their ideas and dreams are more than the stuff of the playground but rather can change communities in meaningful ways.

The authors of each story are to be commended for showing each reader the power and positivity of future generations.

Irina Bokova
Director General of UNESCO

Welcome to the United Arab Emirates!

The author of this story is Kehkashan Basu. She lives in the United Arab Emirates.

Kehkashan is passionate about working for peace and sustainability. She was born on 5th June, which is also World Environment Day, so she feels that she just had to grow up to be an eco-warrior.

Kehkashan founded a youth organisation called Green Hope Foundation, which works to help the environment. It now has over 1,000 members across the Middle East, India, Brazil, USA and Canada!

Kehkashan enjoys singing, reading, travelling, writing, painting and playing the piano and guitar.

THE TREE OF HOPE
Kehkashan Basu

In a small village on the edge of a vast, harsh desert lived a little girl, Khadra, and her mother. The sun beat down unforgivingly on her village from early morning until night, soaking up all the moisture. The heat was especially unforgiving in the middle of the day and drove everyone indoors.

Like any other little girl, Khadra hated being cooped up inside the house and wanted desperately to play outside with her friends, but her mother would have none of it. She was afraid that Khadra would get heat stroke if she spent the afternoon outside.

So, Khadra spent the long afternoons staring out of the window at the undulating sands which shimmered in the heat-haze, and waiting for dusk so that she could go out and play.

She longed for the weather to change so that she could spend more time outdoors. She loved her home and village but wished that it was a little less hot and sunny. Little did she realise that very soon she would have the answer to her dreams.

One morning, Khadra was woken up early by her mother, who asked her to go to the village well to fetch water. Water was very precious in their village and the single well at the village square was its only source.

Every day, there were long queues of residents at the well, waiting for a turn to haul up their daily requirement of water. On that day, Khadra's mother asked her to go early and get

 7

some water because she was expecting a guest at their house and wanted to finish cooking in time for his arrival.

It was a chore which Khadra enjoyed as she met most of her friends at the well. She also loved the splashy sound of water and its cool, soothing feel. The well was very deep and looked a bit scary as she peered over the parapet.

That day, she hurriedly collected the water, slung the bucket on her back and hurried back home as she, too, was excited at the prospect of meeting the guest. Khadra did not really know who he was, except that he was her mother's distant cousin who was a traveller of sorts. Khadra loved to listen to stories, especially of distant, exotic, faraway lands, and she hoped that her visiting uncle would have a tale or two for her.

Khadra's uncle finally arrived in the hot afternoon, carrying a very big bag on his back. He had a craggy but friendly face with the most twinkly eyes Khadra had ever seen. Kahdra was very intrigued by him.

She couldn't wait for their meal to be over, as she wanted to hear stories of her uncle's travels. She was also very curious to find out what was inside her uncle's heavy bag which he had placed carefully by the door. Finally, they finished lunch and her mother went into the kitchen to clean up, warning Khadra to not pester her uncle and to allow him to rest.

Her uncle smiled at the crestfallen look on Khadra's face and whispered to her that he wasn't really tired and would love to chat with her. Delighted, Khadra started asking him to tell her about his most recent adventures.

Her uncle said that he had been to another part of the world which had the most amazing forests and trees. He described how, many years ago, that part of the world was also barren and dry, much like Khadra's village, but somehow the local people had found a way of changing all that.

They had found a plant which could grow and flourish with very little water. Every time there was a happy occasion, like a birthday or a wedding, they planted a sapling to celebrate the event.

The intention was to encourage people to plant more trees. Soon, over time, the whole area became green. As if to prove his point, Khadra's uncle asked her to bring his bag. Telling her to be careful, he invited her to open it. With excited fingers, Khadra untied the strings, and to her surprise there was a small sapling in a pot. The plant had very strange leaves... thick and leathery.

Her uncle said that the leaves were amazing and they stored water. This was the plant's speciality. The plant was capable of saving every drop of available water from its surroundings, thus enabling it to survive long periods of drought. Khadra's uncle said that this tree was a gift from him to her. He told her that her name meant green in Arabic and that maybe she was destined to be the person to seed her village's landscape with the colour green.

Khadra was overjoyed. This was the most exotic gift she had ever received. She gave her uncle a big hug and ran to her mother to share her excitement.

 10

Before he left, her uncle explained to Khadra how to plant and take care of the tree. He told her to find a place in her back yard which was in the shade and to plant it there. He also told Khadra to save a mug of water from her bath every day and use it to water the plant. It needed very little water, he explained, as it survived on the morning dew.

As he departed, he reminded Khadra that once the tree had grown, she should collect the seeds from the plant's fruits. He told her to give these seeds to her friends on their birthdays, and to encourage them to also plant the trees. He hoped Khadra would take on the responsibility to live up to her name.

That evening, Khadra gathered her friends in her back yard and narrated to them the events of the afternoon. She showed them the plant which she had been given by her uncle. Together they dug a hole and planted the sapling.

Time passed and Khadra's sapling flowered and grew into a large, imposing tree. Its branches and leaves offered shade during even the harshest of summers. No longer did Khadra have to stay cooped up indoors during the afternoons. She, along with her friends, spent happy hours sitting under the tree's shade or up in its leafy branches.

Birds that had never before been seen in the village miraculously appeared and nested in the tree. Their morning songs now woke Khadra up every day.

Following her uncle's instructions, her friends plucked the tree's berries and planted the seeds in their own back yards.

The village elders looked on indignantly at the children's antics, with some shaking their heads as if to say that it was all a waste of time. No one noticed at first, but soon it did seem as if the evenings were becoming cooler. Some of the villagers even saw clouds on the horizon – something which had not been seen in many years.

The back yard of each house in the village now had one or more trees, in various stages of bloom, each cared for by one of the children.

Khadra could no longer see the harsh desert sands from her room's back window. Her tree of hope, with its lush green foliage and chirping birds, offered a beautiful green vista instead.

Then, finally, the unthinkable happened: storm clouds filled up the sky and heavy drops of rain splattered on the parched earth. The whole village came out to feel the rain water wash away the dust and sand grains which had engulfed the villagers for so long.

Khadra and her friends danced for joy and drank the cool rain water until they could drink no more. Then Khadra ran to her tree and hugged its trunk tightly to say thank you. It had changed her village into an oasis. It was indeed the tree of hope which had converted a barren land into a living green landscape.

Welcome to Canada!

The author of this story is Jona David. He lives in Canada and also Cambridge, UK, where he studies at King's College School. He is Canadian, British, Swiss and German.

When Jona was seven, he was told he had dyslexia. He was determined to overcome it by memorising the 8,000 most common words in English, and he wrote his first story as a way of proving he had done so. He has now written several books, won awards, and has had his writing translated into four languages.

Along with his little brother Nico, Jona volunteers as a UN Child Ambassador, and has spoken at important conferences all round the world.

Jona enjoys writing, flute, polo, particle physics, chess, maths and studying nature in the wild.

THE EPIC
ECO-INVENTIONS
Jona David

Chapter 1

In a house by a lake in a very green town, there lived a boy and his little brother. Secretly, the boy was a mad genius inventor. But no one knew this – not even his little brother at first. The boy told no one about his inventions. He did not want them to be scared or to laugh at him.

His parents would sometimes tell him off when he came home with strange stains and tears in his clothes. Once, they even found a large piece of delphiniorite (which was an element he had just discovered) in his sports bag.

The boy and his little brother went to what the neighbours called, 'a terribly good school'. They studied: maths, astrophysics, acrobatics, chemistry and biology, care of endangered species, virtual reality programming, telescope repair, geography, archery, music and gargoyle maintenance.

They also studied lots and lots of languages. The boy's little brother was joyful. He loved music and spoke many languages.

For birthdays and other celebrations, the little brother received many toys from his big brother. At first, he did not realise that they were special. He thought his big brother had found his presents in the toy shops! He got...

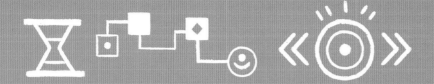

1. A pet robot spider that turns invisible.

BLUEPRINT NOTES: PET ROBOT SPIDER
- Force-field to bend light for invisibility effect
- Positronic brain
- Tiny nebula gas fuel cells
- Special steel and crazy glue web spinner

FORCE-FIELD

WEB SPINNER

FUEL

100%

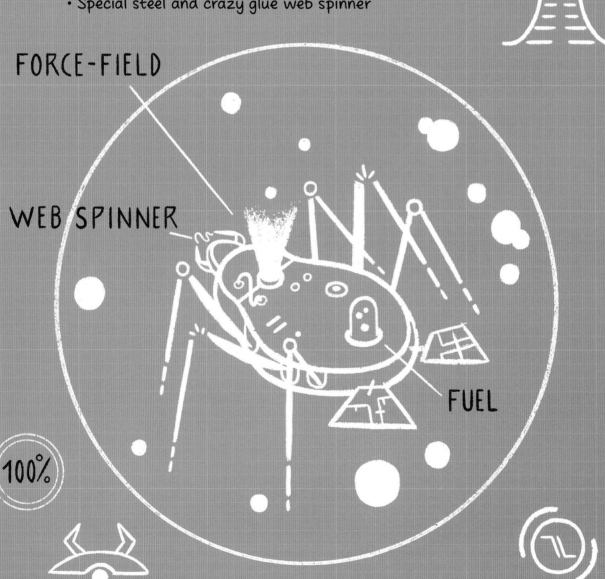

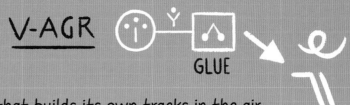

GLUE

2. An anti-gravity train that builds its own tracks in the air.

BLUEPRINT NOTES: ANTI-GRAVITY TRAIN
- Super light hyper-plastic
- Nanotech rods that rebuild and fold track
- Remote-control pointer for directing train
- Nebula gas fuel cells

INVISIBILITY

3. An ultra-light eco-spaceship that paints words on the ceiling.

BLUEPRINT NOTES: ECO-SPACESHIP
- Spray paint (evaporating ink)
- Super-cooled ink tank (non-evaporating)
- Positronic robot brain with language components
- Nebula gas fuel cells

4. A light-maze that makes organic sweets.

BLUEPRINT NOTES: LIGHT MAZE
- Transparent glass for laser-guiding tubes
- Circular base and sweet maker
- Delphiniorite and hyper-plastic for positronic scrambler unit
- Nebula gas, metal and delphiniorite glass

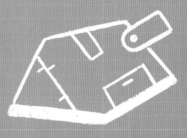

At school, the children loved the little brother's stories about his presents. Everyone thought the stories just came from his imagination. Everyone, that is, apart from the school bully.

Chapter 2

On their first day after Christmas holidays, the boys had their maths, science and English lessons.

The little brother's pet robot spider had followed him to school – but he didn't realise, because it was invisible. The spider robot went to all his classes. It particularly liked gymnastics.

When the little brother and his little friends were on their way home, the spider appeared and did some tricks for them. But when the school bully saw the robot spider, he threatened them and it. The little ones were scared, but they tried to be brave. They called for help.

Luckily, the mad genius inventor boy saw that his little brother was in trouble. Quickly, he activated a force field watch that he had just invented. It spun out, acting as a shield, driving the bully away. The friends were amazed!

For the first time, the little brother started to see that

maybe his toys were rather… unusual.

After the bully had been driven away, the brothers invited their brave friends for a picnic. They took their canoe out to an island in the middle of the lake. They had a great time there, playing hide-and-seek with the pet robot spider.

While they played, the little brother noticed a lever on the side of the island's apple tree. 'I'll come back soon and investigate', he thought.

Chapter 3

The inventor boy had a habit of disappearing for hours at a time, especially in the early mornings when everyone else was asleep.

The little brother decided to investigate the lever in the tree. So one afternoon, after school, he and his pet robot spider snuck away. When he got to the tree, he pulled the lever.

A secret door opened up, with a marvellous glass elevator leading underground. As the little brother went deep into the Earth, a huge laboratory became visible. It was full of physics, chemistry and biology equipment, as well as many half-built inventions.

There were…

1. Personal jet-packs with solar propellors.

BLUEPRINT NOTES: JET PACKS

- Solar propellors for recharging while flying
- Control belt for direction
- Special sun-protection goggles with infra-red for night flying
- Hydro-dynamic underwater mode, with retractable scuba gear

SPECIAL GOGGLES

CONTROL BELT

(UNDERWATER MODE)

SOLAR PROPELLORS

2. A lightning re-charger that could charge non-electrical things.

BLUEPRINT NOTES: LIGHTNING RE-CHARGER

- Lightning meltdown protector shells
- Calibrator energy field matcher to avoid circuit burnout
- Weather vane lightning attractor
- Lightning storage cells

SCUBA GEAR

3. A magma drill that uses geothermal power
for construction projects.

BLUEPRINT NOTES: GEOTHERMAL MAGMA DRILL
- Delphiniorite and diamond super-hard mobile drill-head
- Hyper-sonic boosters to soften materials prior to drilling
- Magma heat treatment to soften rock
- Geothermal super-conductor roots for power source

4. A zoo of mechanical animals that can
build their own nano-habitats.

BLUEPRINT NOTES: NANO-ZOO
- Force-fields for habitats
- Nano-tech frame and tiny coloured marbles
  for building habitats inside globes
- Basic positronic units for learning dances,
  sounds and habitat-building skills

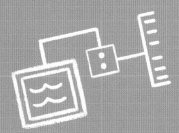

There was even a special nebula gas fuel cell invention. The fuel cell machine, which looked like a large computer with a satellite dish, could directly harness energy from the universe and store it in renewable energy cells, with clouds of swirling purple light.

Suddenly, everything made sense to the little brother. The brilliant toys... his brother's disappearances... their home's never-ending power supply... and the special dashboard on their family hybrid car that read 'flight mode'!

The little boy was astonished. He realised his brother was a mad genius inventor boy!

In one corner of the underground lab there was a strange trampoline-like platform. When the little brother and his pet robot spider climbed up on it, the bounce made them float. It was a disguised anti-gravity machine.

The more they explored, the more they saw. One wall had

a giant control panel, with screens and millions of buttons saying things like 'activate force field'.

Suddenly, the spider activated its chirp alarm. They heard footsteps – someone was coming.

Chapter 4

The hatch opened and the mad genius inventor boy appeared. When he saw his little brother, he laughed. 'I guess I couldn't keep all this secret for ever,' he said.

Then the inventor boy showed his brother the tunnel he had come from. It was long and dark and it led right underneath the lake.

The tunnel came up under their own home, in the cupboard under the stairs. But while the boys were exploring, an awful thing happened.

The school bully had taken a horribly loud motor boat out on the lake. When he saw the little brother's canoe, he stopped at the island to look for him.

He looked around for a while, and then he saw a secret hatch in the grass. When the bully saw the underground lab, he decided that all the amazing inventions could be used as weapons.

He wanted to sell the new technologies to evil dictators to start new wars around the world. So he stuffed all the inventions into a big sack, and started to climb.

Luckily, the inventor boy had not left his lab unprotected.

An alarm sounded and lights came on. A special gravity force field came down like a heavy weight, slowing down the bully-thief so he could barely take a step.

Just as the bully struggled to the top of the ladder, the little brother's pet spider darted forward. He threw out his web, like a bolt of silver lightning, and tangled up the bully-thief. The bully fell to the ground, totally trapped.

Soon the inventor boy and his little brother arrived, alerted by the alarm. They took the bully-thief straight to the police. He was given a warning and agreed to do community service so he could learn to be a better person.

Chapter 5

The mad genius inventor boy, his little brother and their happy pet robot spider headed home in their canoe. They decided it was time to tell everyone about the inventions.

The little brother was worried that if they did not share them, others might steal them and use them for evil. 'It's worth being laughed at if your inventions can help clean up the earth and end poverty,' he said.

When they shared them, everyone was amazed. Their parents even ran out and got patents for everything to protect the mad genius inventor boy's work.

Then the little brother packed the renewable energy machine, the anti-gravity trampoline, the invisibility gadget, and many other eco-toys for children into a large, sturdy suitcase.

During the holidays, the little brother travelled the world, using his knowledge of many languages to share the inventor boy's technologies with leaders of countries who wanted peace and a clean environment.

Many schools were working to start new environmental education programmes, as a clean environment is every child's human right.

They were very pleased to see the little brother and the inventions, because he was so joyful, and the inventions were so clever and useful for learning about eco-science and technology.

Meanwhile, the inventor boy was hard at work in his lab on his next ideas, and people all over the planet were using his new green inventions to learn and live better.

The inventor boy always asked his little brother when he got home, 'what did you see?' and the little brother always answered, 'Oh... the future, the future we want.'

Welcome to Taiwan!

The author of this story is Kuo Yu Yin (Anna). She lives in Taiwan.

Anna likes to learn languages, write and do research. She hopes that her writing can express the ideas of looking after resources, caring for the environment, and working towards world peace – so that future generations can live in a more sustainable, better world.

When she grows up, Anna hopes to be a doctor or a writer.

She also enjoys reading, swimming and travelling.

THE FIREFLIES AFTER THE TYPHOON

Anna Kuo

Chapter 1

On top of a small hill, in the mountains on the island of Formosa, lay the beautiful Peach Blossom Village. Rare animals roamed the hills of the village. Macaques swung from one tree to another, Formosan sika deer showed their pretty spots, Mikado pheasants made special 'ke ke ke' calls, Taiwanese hwamei laughingthrush birds flew with startled eyebrows, and squirrels and rabbits also ran about. They were happy in their forest habitats around the village. Flowers and trees blossomed everywhere and Anodendron vines bloomed beautiful with flowers every spring.

The villagers led peaceful lives in harmony with their surroundings. The children, especially, spent a lot of time in the forest – it was their playground, their school and their foraging ground. They often gathered nuts, fruits and mushrooms to give to their families and to share with their neighbours.

They loved to watch in the evenings as the fireflies danced among the trees, their little lanterns lighting the deep, dark green of the forest shadows with cheerful signals of life and love.

A boy named Tongyan grew up in this green, lively environment. He was a respectful and quiet boy, curious and interested in everything that grew, but often solemn. He

31

usually got along with everyone at school because he did not argue, but he felt happiest in the forest.

Every day, after school, he would explore the woods and streams with his friends, observing the life cycles of all the special animals and plants living in balance with each other and their surroundings. All seemed well until one fateful day.

Chapter 2

At first, it seemed just like any other day. Tongyan had finished school and was thinking about whether to catch a caterpillar for his nature studies or to play a game of 'beggar ticks' with his classmates, after doing his homework.

As he walked home, Tongyan suddenly noticed many workers moving quickly through the forest, clearing the large and shady trees that once stood tall and proud. The cut raw logs were being loaded onto trucks and driven away.

This was a horrifying sight for Tongyan. 'Why are they cutting down all our special trees? Where will the animals and insects live if the trees are cut down?' Tongyan asked himself in shock.

When he arrived home, he found his parents discussing important matters in low, serious voices at the low table on

 32

their veranda. Tongyan wanted to ask what they were talking about and approached them respectfully. Before he could even raise his question, his parents turned to him. 'Go and do your homework quietly,' they ordered, 'we have to tell you something serious, after dinner.'

Tongyan did not understand why he was being sent away and why his parents were so secretive. However, he was a good boy and knew not to let curiosity get the better of him. He went to his room to work on his maths, science and Chinese studies, as he had been told.

After dinner, Tongyan sat with his family in the living room and they stared at each other without a word. His parents had a solemn, serious look on their faces. It was his father who broke the spell of silence. He said, 'You must have noticed many men, cutting down all of our village forests as you walked home today.' Tongyan nodded.

Then his father said, 'We have now resolved to plant betel palms. The village elders have held a long discussion about this, over the last few weeks. We all have money problems in this village and they want better lives for ourselves and our families.

'This may mean that you cannot play outside in nature with your friends like you used to in the woods, but so long as we take good care of those betel palms, they say, we will be able to make more money and buy many things for ourselves.'

Tongyan was a respectful boy. He did not argue or say anything. Deep inside, he was sad and confused by the decision. He could not understand why some village men had decided to harm and take away his wildlife friends, his playground, and his discoveries, just for the sake of being able to buy more things.

Chapter 3

Three years passed and the children watched as the diverse wildlife of Peach Blossom Village was almost completely replaced by a productive, industrial monoculture of straight, stiff betel palms. The palms stuck out of the primly tended soil like rows of spiky toothbrushes.

The village adults had new jobs, working in the plantations, keeping everything growing in straight rows and harvesting the betel palms. Betel palms produce betel nuts. Some say that betel nuts can protect your body and keep your spirits up, so many folks eat them. That's why planting betel palms can make a lot of money.

Unfortunately, Tongyan and the people of the village could no longer hear the birds singing in spring, could no longer smell the fragrance of blooming flowers and could no longer see children dashing off to play and make hideouts in the forests. The children mainly stayed indoors, watching their new televisions or playing video games.

The streams were fierce yet sullen, carrying chemicals for growing palms away from the village and over the rocks. People had begun to worry about whether they should drink the water. Some neighbours living downstream complained that the water was making them ill. The children were very sad. Their hideouts were felled or forbidden.

They gathered in corners at school and spoke in quiet voices about the loss of their forests and about the unfairness of the choice that had been made without their views being heard. They missed their forest friends, especially the dancing lights of the fireflies at dusk.

The typhoons and heavy rains became worse each year. They knocked over trees, blocked mountain paths and destroyed the roads that the villagers needed. Another major typhoon was approaching. The village elders heard the early warning alerts and knew that people could not simply stay in their homes when they are right in the path of such a serious typhoon.

At first, the villagers were grateful for their new televisions and radios, which gave them warnings and updates about the storm as it got closer. They were all advised to evacuate to emergency shelters at the foot of the mountain before the typhoon arrived.

Tongyan and his parents packed as many of their belongings as they could and then travelled down to the shelter. They were careful and arrived in good time, before the storm got too bad.

The gloom of the storm clouds was heavy all afternoon. Soon, the mighty typhoon could be seen travelling towards them, speeding across the sky. The force of the typhoon struck hardest at night. Its powerful winds and downpours destroyed every road connecting the village to the rest of the island. The vegetation covering the earth was ripped away mercilessly.

The villagers hiding in the shelter looked at each other,

knowing that their homes, the things they had bought with the betel money and all that they had worked to build might be broken up or blown away.

But that wasn't the worst thing to happen to the village. All the people of the island had expected to get back to their lives, once the typhoon left, having blown over on its way past them to China. No one foresaw the serious landslide that was to come right afterwards.

A torrent of roaring mud, gravel and stone swept down through the village, bringing many giant boulders with it that crushed everything in their path. There was nothing the villagers could do against the force of nature. They could only look on helplessly from their tiny shelter, as the boulders rolled over their houses like a mass of angry, stampeding animals. The noise of destruction shook them to their very souls.

Peach Blossom Village suffered from the typhoon's destruction. A devastated landscape greeted the refugees leaving the shelter. Homes, fields, their new clinic, their old school and their traditional community centre were completely buried beneath mud and debris. No one could see any hope for their future. Tongyan and all the children were angry and very worried. They felt powerless and lost. What could they do to rebuild their homes? How could they find a new future?

Chapter 4

The entire village, including the elders, the parents and the children, felt dusty, sad and tired. Tongyan ran out to the big stone that stood where the school had once been and found his friends waiting there. The children talked and talked.

They believed that the terrible impact of the disaster was a result of planting the betel palms. 'Our teachers explained that in the UN Convention on the Rights of the Child,' Tongyan said slowly, 'everyone recognises that we have a right to education about nature and that this right should be respected.'

 38

An older child added, 'This is how we know that the decision of our village council, three years ago, taken without thinking about the future, has caused terrible things.' They remembered that they had learned in school about palm trees' shallow root systems, which were poorly adapted to holding the soil together. 'There's no way those toothbrushes could hold up against the landslides,' said another child.

Tongyan then began to wonder out loud. 'In the same Convention, it says that we have a right to a clean environment and that our needs should be taken into account when adults make choices for us. I am not sure these two rights have been respected.' He added, 'Our parents, even us children, knew that the decision of the elders was not right. But we did not ask questions and we kept quiet. We must help out and find a good way to share our views.' The children resolved, together, to make a change in the way the village did things. They wanted to be a part of decision-making and they needed their voices to be heard.

Tongyan spoke seriously to his parents: 'In our eyes, planting all those betel palms for money has led to many terrible losses. It has destroyed our wonderful forests and our friends, as well as everything that we built and bought. If only we had planned for the future rather than cutting down so much, so fast, maybe we would not face this disaster today.'

Tongyan's parents listened and then spoke to their fellow villagers. The older men who had made decisions alone were worried. They reflected upon the parents' and the children's words. They agreed that their decision to grow betel palms was a very bad choice. Everyone decided to correct this mistake and work together to rebuild Peach Blossom Village so that it could develop sustainably.

Chapter 5

Happy voices rang out and visitors wandered towards the new village centre, where the school and playground had been rebuilt. 'These colourful flower beds and climbing vines are amazing!' said one visitor. 'We can't even tell that this village has been restored after a disaster!' replied another. 'Hush! Are those Swinhoe's pheasants and Taiwan blue magpies? They're very rare,' called another, as she stepped off a forest canopy trail.

This beautiful village with many visitors was the reconstructed Peach Blossom Village. The villagers had decided to replant native trees and plants that were beneficial to their local environment. They had dedicated themselves to restoring the forest, so that the animals that once lived around their village could return to their homes.

They grew colourful hanging gardens and invited eco-tourists to stay with them in order to see rare species of plants, animals and birds, and to learn Chinese. The villagers also held special races and festivals according to their old traditions. Students from many lands came to visit and to help. Everyone kept the grave lesson about harming an ecosystem in their hearts and agreed to care for their environment together, working towards the future they wanted.

Tongyan and the other children had become a part of the process in a children's council. They helped as they could, giving their ideas and a new point of view. They even made a new special hideout in the forest and nicknamed it 'Paradise of New Hope.'

They gathered just before dusk and, when their parents called from the verandas, they walked back slowly towards their homes, trailing their fingers backwards among the leaves. On arriving home, Tongyan said, 'Look, Mother! Our forest fireflies are back, dancing and blinking in the dark!'

Welcome to South Africa

The author of this story is Diwa Boateng. He lives in South Africa.

Diwa's story is inspired by his own research into the different lives of rich and poor people in the African countries he knows best – South Africa, where he was born; Ghana, where his father is from; and Zimbabwe and Zambia, where his mother grew up and where members of his family still live.

As well as being an eco-warrior, Diwa is a computer designer and cartoon animator, and loves reading.

His story is dedicated to his grandparents who always encouraged him to study hard.

THE FORWARD AND
BACKWARD CITY
Diwa Boateng

Chapter 1

It is 2030 and Kabwe is playing with his hand-held Infin8r machine at school. He has heard from his father that in the year 2000, schools used to have blackboards and actual teachers with textbooks and chalk.

Kabwe tries to imagine what this must have been like but he can't – all he knows is that it must have been soooo boring. He is just thankful that he has a virtual library, a virtual teacher, and a virtual pen and paper, and that school is such fun.

Kabwe lives with his mother and father in the savannah grasslands of Africa, in the beautiful city of Madini. Madini is a bright city built on top of many precious minerals. The Tibela River divides the city into Madini North and Madini South. Kabwe lives in Madini North. It is ultra-modern. It is built using the latest advanced technology.

Kabwe's father is the Mayor of Madini. They live in a castle on the top of a hill in the centre of the city. The castle roof is made of gold, with door-knobs of polished diamonds. The family eats from emerald plates with platinum forks and knives. They drink from rhodium goblets. Their baths are made of titanium and they bathe in mineral-rich spring water. Their food, including vegetables, is all genetically enhanced to make it more juicy, nutritious and healthy. They have many servants and many gadgets which do everything for them.

There is only one problem: Kabwe is an only child and he is very lonely. He has grown tired of his Infin8r and longs to have someone real to play with. He also loves to read but he only has a few collector's item paperback and hardback children's story books. He can only read them at the weekend when he is resting from all his technology.

He stacks them on his bedroom windowsill. His window is always open because the gadgets and minerals make the house very hot. Kabwe has a secret wish – he keeps his window open all day and night because he prays that an imaginary friend will come and find him one day.

Chapter 2

All the servants working in the castle come from the other part of the city, Madini South, where life is tough. There is no pure water and big families cram themselves into small houses.

They only eat some porridge and fish from the river, once a day. Parents leave home early in the morning to work. Some work in houses and castles like Kabwe's. Others go fishing and sell fish, iced water, groundnuts and other wares at the roadside. There are no schools in this part of the city because the money for classrooms and books is spent in Madini North, Kabwe's part of the city. But there is lots of room to play in the dust, even until sundown.

The children in this part of the city have many friends and they create their own games and toys: cars and aeroplanes made of wire, cans and plastic bottles. They invent stick-fighting martial arts games and board games using cardboard and smooth stones.

They have turned the inside and outside walls of their houses into picture murals of the future they want to see. This future has schools, teachers and books, roads, clean water, hospitals and lots of food. They also imagine having toys and educational gadgets to play with. Above all, they wish they could also live in big houses like the people in Madini North do.

Chapter 3

One of the servants in Kabwe's house is a happy woman called Shamiso. She is a struggling widow with six children. She leaves them early every morning to go to work at Kabwe's house.

She loves him like her own son and does everything for

him: cooking, cleaning, bathing him, and other things he could actually do by himself.

Every day she tells him about her son Tatenda who is also nine years old and who was born on the same day as Kabwe. She shares stories about the creative toys Tatenda makes to play with. When she goes home every night, she tells Tatenda and her other children about Kabwe and all his gadgets.

Every night at bedtime, the powerful technological light beams from Kabwe's castle on the hill bounce off the Tibela River and shine into Tatenda's dark home. One Saturday night, Tatenda has to go to bed hungry and he cannot sleep. He is missing his best friend Sahwira.

Sadly, an epidemic has been sweeping the land. Sahwira has to leave the city and return to his village with his family to take care of his aunties, uncles and cousins who live there. Tatenda is worried because he does not know when or if his best friend will come back to the city.

He also cannot hold in his curiosity about Kabwe any longer so he decides to sail his father's rickety kayak to Kabwe's home. He climbs the hill and finds Kabwe's bedroom window open with the stack of books on the windowsill.

He overhears the mayor and his wife yawning as they tell Kabwe that they are going to bed and he should finish playing with his Infin8r soon and sleep too.

Tatenda takes a deep breath and sneaks into the bedroom through the open window.

He borrows a very interesting looking book from the pile on Kabwe's windowsill and puts it in his rucksack. He makes his way to the kitchen, hoping to rummage for food. He opens what looks like a fridge and he can't believe all the kinds of delicious food he finds!

As Tatenda is about to bite into a piece of juicy chicken, he suddenly hears footsteps coming towards him. He starts to panic and sweat beads on his brow and prickles his armpits. It is too late to run. He freezes when a boy who fits Shamiso's description of Kabwe points a flashlight at him and threaten

to set off the alarm with the remote in his hand. It is Kabwe and although he is also scared, he boldly asks Tatenda, 'Who are you?'

'Please. It's Ta-ta-tenda... I am Sh-Shamiso's son. I live in the other part of the city. I am very hungry. Please forgive me. Sorry...' Tatenda replies as he drops the piece of chicken. The boys stare at each other nervously and are unsure of what to do or say next. They stand and stare at each other with hearts beating loudly in the awkward silence.

To Kabwe, Tatenda looks thinner but taller than he had imagined from Shamiso's stories. Kabwe thinks Tatenda's clothes look like a ragged and dirty uniform and his hair looks very coiled and hard, like it has never been combed. Tatenda also smells a bit sweaty but Kabwe thinks that this must be because of fear and the heat in the house.

To Tatenda, Kabwe seems rounder, shorter and more plump than he had imagined from Shamiso's stories. He is dressed like a prince in the best African silk and linen pyjamas with fine, soft leather sandals. Just as Tatenda is trying to think of what to say, the book falls out of his rucksack. Kabwe's face lights up because he thinks the book, which he loves, belongs to Tatenda and that they must have something in common. They both bend down to pick up the book and bump their heads. They smile nervously into each others' eyes and their

smiles warmly soften the tense atmosphere. Kabwe breaks the silence by asking how Tatenda got into the house and they end up spending hours getting to know each other. Tatenda confesses to having borrowed Kabwe's book and the next thing they know, they are best friends.

Kabwe offers Tatenda some sweet water to drink and fills the table with a lot of food. Kabwe eats until he is too full. They then spend several hours looking at all Kabwe's toys and gadgets.

Langa, a friend of Tatenda's from Madini South, had a gadget but it was made in 2012 and it is worn out from over-use. Langa generously lent it to everyone. When Kabwe demonstrates how the cyber world of the Infin8r works, tears well up in Tatenda's eyes. He tries to hide them, but a big one falls onto the screen of the Infin8r.

He explains to Kabwe that where he comes from, children do not get these kinds of gadgets and toys. Kabwe is shocked and devastated to hear that they do not even have schools. He cannot believe that there are no school resources in Madini South, when he and his classmates have left old versions of their Infin8rs lying around. These wasted gadgets would still be perfectly useful but are now gathering dust in basements and sheds all over Madini North.

Speaking of his home reminds Tatenda that it is time for him to go back. Kabwe fills Tatenda's rucksack with bottles of sweet water, lots of chicken, fruit and delicious vegetables to take home. Tatenda leaves feeling happy that his family will be eating something other than fish for the next few days.

Chapter 5

Kabwe goes to bed knowing that he will have to talk to his father about building schools in Tatenda's part of the city. When his parents wake up, he tells them about Tatenda and what he said. His father is worried about how Tatenda made it into the house but he is more shocked about the plight of the children in Madini South. He is angry because the deputy mayor and his team have always been in charge of Tatenda's area.

The mayor checks his Infin8r for information and finds statements from the deputy mayor showing the number of schools, hospitals, water treatment plants and houses which have supposedly been built in Madini South in the last five years. Kabwe says he believes Tatenda and that nothing was actually done at all. Kabwe's father believes his son.

That week, the mayor carries out what he calls a special, forensic financial investigation on what the deputy mayor has been doing. He finds that the deputy mayor and his team have been keeping all the money that was meant for Tatenda and the other families for themselves.

They have used it to buy a fleet of highly technologically advanced and customised Cheetah cars, which move at 300km an hour, and have hidden them in secret garages. They have equipped their houses with robots which do everything for them.

Shockingly, the deputy mayor's wife has been bathing in milk and using gold dust as make-up. The deputy mayor has also filled a special bunker with vaults of cash. It seems the list of selfish and unfair things done with the money is endless.

The mayor is very angry and sad because this has left Tatenda and other people to suffer.

After the investigation is completed, the mayor decides to hold a ceremony to honour Tatenda's bravery in exposing the problems in the city. The mayor's speech at the ceremony mentions something called the UN Convention on the Rights of the Child, from many years ago, which says all children should have an education, clean water, a clean environment, a right to play, a right to be heard and lots of other nice things.

Tatenda cannot believe his ears that there is such a global promise and he cannot wait to find out about it. Just as Tatenda is daydreaming about the Convention, he is asked to come to the podium. To his complete surprise the mayor says that Tatenda is being appointed as a junior mayor for his part of the city. Before he can figure out what this means, there is a large roar of applause and he is being draped

in a heavy gold chain with lots of medallions which look like large coins.

He is also handed a custom-made rhodium walking stick with the symbol of Madini, a large lion's face. The mayor calls it the mayoral mace. While Tatenda is admiring the lion's head, he is also handed a thick golden envelope with a golden seal of the face of a lion. As Tatenda stands there in the midst of the applause, he knows that this all means his life will never be the same.

After the ceremony, Tatenda and his family are invited to the mayor's castle on the hill for a feast. The mayor, his wife and Kabwe are dressed as waiters and they serve Tatenda's family. Everyone thinks this is funny but they, especially Shamiso, feel very important for the first time.

To crown the day, the mayor makes sure that Tatenda and his family are taken home in the mayor's official yacht. Even Tatenda's older brothers are being extra nice to him that night. Tatenda can't believe all the things that have happened today. It is the best day of his life and he only wishes that his best friend Sahwira could have been there beside him.

Just before bed, he remembers to open the envelope. It is written on official paper which is embossed with the Madini lion. This is what the letter says:

Dear Tatenda Gambia,

The city of Madini would like to congratulate you for uncovering corruption. In recognition of your efforts, the city of Madini is pleased to appoint you junior mayor of the area South of Madini. This means you will be responsible for investigating whether the children in Madini South are enjoying the rights they have been guaranteed in the UN Convention on the Rights of the Child. The Convention is enclosed with this letter.

Please read and understand it as it will be your investigative guide. Please find a team of girls and boys to help you in your investigations.

You will report all your findings to me, the Mayor of Madini, during a special meeting at my offices every month. I look forward to working with you.

Well done and congratulations!
Yours Faithfully,

The Mayor of Madini

Signed on this 15th day of February 2030
in the city of Madini.

It is bedtime but Tatenda is joyful, excited and shocked. He can't believe this is really happening to him. He has trouble sleeping because so many thoughts are competing for his attention. He is thinking about who he can invite to join his team, what investigations they will carry out, how they will work, whether they should have uniforms and so many other things.

He really wishes that instead of being out fighting the terrible epidemic in the countryside, Sahwira would come back soon and help him. Just then, he remembers that he will have to study this Convention document which is in the letter. It looks long and important, with many articles, but he knows that since he loves reading, he will study it very hard.

Before he falls asleep, he imagines the new future he will have now that the corruption scheme has been uncovered. Although he is lying on a small bed with two of his brothers, he imagines that, in the future, he will live in a home with adequate space and that all families in Madini South will have healthy food and water and hopefully medicine to fight epidemics. He breathes a sigh of relief and drifts off into a deep, restful sleep, dreaming about his bright future.

Welcome to
Papua New Guinea!

The author of this story is Tyronah Sioni. She is originally from Papua New Guinea and lives in Singapore.

Most of all, Tyra loves helping the planet. She hopes one day to create a worldwide charity called Evergreen. Her charity will help people in need, especially those who can't afford food and homes. It will also help to tackle environmental problems and reduce pollution.

Tyra also dreams of making the world fairer by uncovering corruption, discrimination and harassment.

She also enjoys singing and dancing.

THE VISIBLE GIRLS
Tyronah Sioni

Chapter 1

There was once a girl named Sine. Sine loved to draw and loved swimming. Sine was a fierce and independent yet friendly girl, who was always ready to help anything or anyone in danger. She loved her island. She lived on a small island a small distance from Port Moresby with her mother, in a small village. It was all they could afford after her father died. She had a best friend named Kaimon, who was the truest, kindest and bravest person she knew. The only trouble with Kaimon was that other people, for some reason, could not see or hear her.

One day, as Sine and Kaimon were getting off the boat that took them to their school on a neighbouring island, they saw something a bit strange. They were passing a shop on the docks. They saw a man shouting at a woman and forcing her out of the shop, until the woman was lying helplessly on the ground. The man looked very selfish and arrogant.

Kaimon nudged Sine, telling her that they simply must do something. Sine trembled a bit but then regained her confidence. She raced over and told the loud man to stop. The woman got up slowly and limped away. Nobody else said anything.

Sine walked the rest of the way to school. She kept thinking about what they had witnessed and how wrong it was. Her mother always told her that respecting other people was very

important. How was it possible that a lady was treated so and that no one would stand up for her but two small girls, one of whom no one could even see?

Chapter 2

After many lessons and much worry, Sine decided to tell her school principal what had happened. The principal was kind and thanked her for talking about it. She explained that violence and discrimination against women and girls is forbidden in the UN Convention on the Rights of the Child. It remained, however, a major problem in many island communities and countries. Sine remembered seeing something on the news about groups who worked to educate people about this problem and helped to find solutions.

That afternoon, Sine threw her school bag over her shoulder and left through the tall front doors of her school with Kaimon. They went straight to the island library to do some further research on the problem of violence and discrimination against women and girls. They learned many things about how women and girls can be mistreated. They began to understand that turning their backs, and pretending to be invisible, was exactly the wrong way to change things.

As Sine went to bed that night, she thought about what the two girls might do. She dreamed that she and Kaimon worked together to create an education programme about Women's Rights. She even saw their motto, 'Women Forever, Girls Together (WFGT)', painted in bright colours on a big banner.

The next day, Sine and Kaimon went straight to their principal's office. Sine asked permission to speak on women's rights and gender equality in their school assembly, as a first step in starting a new children's education radio programme for girls and women. The principal agreed. Sine worked hard to prepare her presentation, taking on more research, and practising with Kaimon, who gave her lots of advice. On the day of her speech, she was very nervous. Kaimon encouraged her, telling her to be brave. They had to do something, after all. And since Sine was visible, the task of speaking out was hers! Sine wished that Kaimon could also have a voice and be seen so that she could help. But she knew it was impossible.

During assembly, Sine felt alone at first, but she spoke in a clear voice. She explained that women do have rights and should be able to live without fear or violence, and to participate without discrimination. She told a story that everyone could understand.

At the end, she encouraged everyone to stand up for their rights. She challenged everyone to help create a new educational programme with her. There were many smiles and nods as she finished. Kaimon cheered the loudest, even though Sine was the only one who could hear her.

The principal, teachers and students agreed to support the new programme. The principal thought it would be a great opportunity for the school, for the students and for the country's development.

Chapter 3

Sine worked hard with her friends to hang up flyers all around the village. The flyers were bright and colourful. They explained all the activities and games they were planning as WFGT education activities. Every day, more and more members joined. Most of them were girls, but after a while, boys also joined.

They started a children's radio programme and held interviews with all the women leaders in their community, asking them questions and seeking ideas for things that girls could do to help improve their village. Kaimon could participate more that way because, even though she was still invisible, her voice was getting stronger. Sometimes, when it was only Sine and Kaimon in the studio, she would speak out about the things she cared about, and people started to hear her.

Before long, even adult women and men were asking if they could join. Sine always said, 'The more, the merrier!' and Kaimon would dance in excitement.

Soon, all the women and most of the men in the village had signed up. They were becoming very active, even starting their own little projects. Many of the girls and women started their own small businesses: growing flowers or vegetables to sell; raising chickens and delivering eggs to families for breakfast; painting pictures and carving sculptures; even making necklaces out of shells. One woman had the idea to begin a tiny new savings bank, so that all the women could borrow money to start their garden or craft businesses, then pay it back to be lent out to help others.

One afternoon, Kaimon and Sine were leading their radio programme and taking calls from girls all over the island who wanted to share stories of their activities. They were playing a song to rest their voices, when the telephone rang.

It was a friend called Tau and he wanted to arrange a meeting with the Prime Minister so that Sine could tell him what the group was doing. Sine felt all nervous again, but Kaimon didn't hesitate. She answered right away: 'That would be awesome!' And then the music ended, so straight away, Sine announced over the radio that the women's rights group would be meeting the Prime Minister. Everyone was surprised, but also very proud. And they knew they couldn't back down now.

Chapter 4

The next morning, Sine and Kaimon woke up early. Sine's mother had made her favourite: bananas and fish! After breakfast, Sine went down to the beach for a bath. She saw her friends in the waters nearby but did not stop to say hello, as her mind was too busy. Sine and Kaimon played in the warm waves together to help each other calm down. They could see leaping silver dolphins just beyond the breakwater, and this filled them with happiness.

When they arrived back at Sine's house, a visitor was waiting. Sine's mother was sitting on the mat in front of him. It was Tau, the friend who had called them on the radio. Tau had very exciting news for Sine and Kaimon – the meeting was arranged and the girls would travel all the way to Port Moresby to meet the Prime Minister of their country.

Sine was terribly excited and nervous all over again. She glanced at Kaimon, asking silently for reassurance. Tau looked too, and then asked Kaimon directly, 'And what would you like to say to the leader of your country, little brave one?' Kaimon smiled and answered gaily, 'I'll just explain that there is strength in all of us. When the girls of Papua New Guinea come together and stand up for each other, we can change the world.' Sine nearly jumped two miles in the air. She was amazed! It was the first time that anyone – except her – had really been able to see Kaimon.

Sine felt her heart fill with joy. She was happy that people were finally recognising their girls' education programme and all the efforts of the group to bring boys and girls together for a better village. And she was surprised but overjoyed that her best friend, who had always been quietly beside her and supporting her, was finally becoming... visible!

The next morning, the girls were woken by the sound of crashing waves. They prepared quickly and Tau knocked on the door an hour later. They stopped at their local market to pick up some supplies, then travelled all the way to Port Moresby. Kaimon laughed and told stories for the whole trip and Sine loved it, because Tau really answered. He could see Kaimon and understand her, too!

Chapter 5

Before they knew it, they had arrived at the Prime Minister's office. Tau pressed the doorbell and stood there with a large grin on his face, while Sine became very nervous again. Kaimon gave her a quick hug in reassurance and then straightened up politely.

The large wooden door opened and a tall thin man, with his nose high up in the air, led them to an elegant office. They quietly entered through the door and approached the Prime Minister. He was sitting comfortably in a large cushiony chair at the end of a bulky, wooden, oval-shaped table in a bright room with lots of certificates and carvings on the wall.

Tau was the first to say hello. Then the Prime Minister turned to Sine and Kaimon, saying welcome. Sine answered with a trembling voice and Kaimon smiled brightly, but said nothing. Sine was terrified that her friend had disappeared again. But the Prime Minister asked both girls to sit down in the chairs diagonally next to him.

He had heard about the WFGT programmes on the radio and he was interested in what they were doing. Sine told him about their mission to improve awareness of women's rights in the community and eventually the whole country. Kaimon added that women are citizens of this planet, too.

The Prime Minister was delighted. He was proud of the girls and everything that they had done. He was also happy because, as he explained, it was his mission to make sure that girls and women never felt frightened or silenced again. He had just been to New York, he explained, to the United Nations, and world leaders had agreed on Sustainable Development Goals for the whole planet.

Gender equality, and participation of girls and women in the community, were two of the most important goals that the world leaders had committed to achieving. 'As soon as I heard your radio programme, I realised that it won't be

as hard as I thought for my country,' he admitted. 'With visible girls like you on our side, we'll meet our goals, and I believe that we'll even have fun doing it!' Kaimon's smile was brilliant and Sine nearly cried for joy. By standing up for themselves and for each other, they could help make the world better for everyone.

Welcome to Mexico!

The author of this story is Allison Hazel Liévano Gómez. She lives in Mexico. Allison is a keen reader and writer. Her favourite author is Malala Yousafzai and she enjoys books from authors as varied as Roald Dahl, Joaquin Salvador Lavado (Quino), J.K. Rowling and Nick Vujicic.

In her stories, Allison draws on her experience of growing up with her older sister Daniela, who has Down Syndrome and autism. Allison is passionate about working for the rights and opportunities of children with disabilities.

Allison has also won an award for robot design! In 2016 she designed and programmed an educational robot and won first place in her category at an international robotics competition.

THE SISTERS'
MIND CONNECTION
Allison Hazel Lievano-Gomez

Chapter 1

Reading a dog's mind is easy: they mostly think about food and cats and fetching balls and rolling on the grass. Reading a human's mind is more difficult. They think about work and are tense, especially adults.

Michelle was very special, kind and gentle. But she couldn't express how she felt by talking because she had a double diagnosis: autism and Down syndrome. Michelle's parents couldn't find an appropriate school for her. Michelle was Clara's big sister. They lived in Mexico City.

Clara was the 'middle of the sandwich'. She was a splendid girl (that's what her mum always said!). She gave all her effort to her work at school and she was also very joyful. She wished that her sister Michelle could talk. She loved Michelle very much.

Clara also has a marvellous little brother called Jorge. He loved programming, coding and building things. He was an inventor. He called his inventions 'Jorge-apps'! He designed computer apps that came alive, like virtual robots, and they really worked. He created an app to feed and clean up after Cafecito, the family's fancy and adorable Chihuahua; an app to pick up his toys; a monster-detector app to look for monsters under his bed; and even a nanorobot app to plant hair on bald heads. Clara's dad really liked that one! There were so many Jorge-apps!

The children were very happy together. They would laugh, sing and dance, and especially liked jumping up and down on the trampoline. They visited the park, where Michelle had a special flowering jacaranda tree that she loved in all seasons and never tired of visiting. They sometimes had fights, but they always worked things out very quickly. They were like magnets: they wanted to be together.

Once, the children visited an amazing fair with big rides and had a fabulous time. Michelle and Clara tried the fastest and splashiest ride, but Jorge was too small for that, so he quickly invented a special floating shoes app, to make himself look taller. He really enjoyed that ride in particular.

Chapter 2

The children also made up their own games. One game they always played together is called 'superpowers'. Jorge and Clara imagined that Michelle had special powers that only they knew about: Michelle could fly or see through walls, and she could hear conversations from very far away. She used these superpowers to help Jorge and Clara to escape from trouble.

Sometimes it really did seem like Michelle had superpowers! Like the time when she found the note 'Doh' on the piano, like magic, after the piano teacher sang the note to her, or the time when she suddenly sang perfectly in front of hundreds of people!

One day, the children's parents finally found a special school for Michelle. Clara was very excited because she thought Michelle would be very happy there. But it did bother her. Clara did not understand why her sister Michelle could not be in the same school as her and Jorge. The three children should be together, in Clara's mind. It would be fantastic, she felt. She dreamt of it.

There was something else that Clara found hard. Every time they played with their neighbours, she noticed that they didn't want to play with Michelle. They didn't understand her. And worse, sometimes they even laughed at her. Clara wanted more people to understand Michelle, not only Jorge and her.

When Michelle came back after her first day at the special school, she seemed to be happy and relaxed. She even seemed proud as she carried her own folders and workbooks up the garden path. But suddenly, she tripped and fell down, dropping all her new schoolwork. Their neighbour, Agatha, laughed in a cruel way, saying to the other children in the neighbourhood, 'She's so dumb!'

Clara was very upset. She thought to herself: 'Why does she act like that with my sister? Why can't people understand Michelle?'

In school, she had learned about the United Nations Convention on the Rights of The Child. Clara knew that children with different abilities have the same rights as other children. It just seemed unfair that this was not happening for her sister. Clara could not sleep that night. She tossed and turned in her bed, worrying and trying to think of a solution. She thought and thought about it, and finally fell asleep.

Chapter 3

The next morning, Clara saw Jorge experimenting with one of his crazy coding projects. He was working on a strange looking headset. She asked him, 'What is that? And what are you doing?' Jorge answered, 'It is a mind-connection app.

It translates the electro-magnetic waves of the brain.' She laughed. 'What a crazy idea!'

Her brother persuaded her to place it on her head. Suddenly, a strange robot-voice said, 'I want pizza.' That was exactly the same thing that Clara had been thinking. She was thrilled. 'It worked! And if the app worked with me...' she thought, '... it would work with Michelle!'

This was the solution! With a mind-connection app, all people would be able to hear what Michelle thought and felt. They would be able to understand her. Clara hugged Jorge and ran out of the room, leaving him looking a bit anxious.

When Michelle came back from school that day, Clara ran down the stairs to give the headset to her. She put the app on Michelle's head and suddenly a sweet voice said, 'Hi Clara!' Clara was very excited and started asking Michelle all the things she had always wanted to ask her. The sisters talked about their vacations together, about their birthday parties, and most of all, they talked about their feelings.

Clara learned many special things about Michelle. She learned that her favourite colour was purple and her favourite food was pasta. She learned that when Michelle flapped her arms, it was because she was excited, and when she screeched her teeth, it meant that she was tired and, when she hummed, she was trying to say that she was hungry. It was all so interesting!

Suddenly, Clara had an idea. She could share the app with Michelle in front of the other kids! She could even organise a party to make new friends for Michelle. They would be able to hear her, and would immediately see that she was a very gentle and kind person.

It would be great! Clara decided to invite all the neighbourhood children and all their friends from school. They could finally understand Michelle! It was an excellent idea! That night Michelle and Clara dreamed happy dreams.

Chapter 4

The next day, Clara woke up at 7am to prepare everything. She was terribly excited. Today was the party! It was Saturday, which was Michelle's favourite day, because on Saturdays the sisters always went to the park together. But Clara told herself that they could always go to the park some other day. Michelle would be happy at the party.

Clara decorated the house, and prepared the music and the food. The decorations were purple, Michelle's favourite colour. All their friends started coming in. Even Agatha, the neighbourhood bully, came. Just then, loud music started to play.

Michelle was the last one to arrive. She was wearing the mind-connection app headset. Clara was delighted to see her. But in that moment, a strange voice from the headset said: 'I need to escape from here. There's too much noise and so many people. I want to go to the park like we always do. There is too much noise! Please get me out!' Michelle started to shout 'Aaaaaaaaaaaaaaaah!' in a high, panicked voice.

Everybody was staring at her and some children were even laughing at her. Finally, Michelle opened the door and ran away so fast that her headset fell off. Clara and Jorge ran after her, but Michelle ran too fast and they could not find her. Luckily, the children's parents also searched. They found Michelle hiding in her special tree and took her carefully around to the back entrance to the house and into her room.

Clara looked down and saw the headset, lying broken on the garden path. She looked back and all the sisters' friends were still dancing happily inside the house. Then she ran to tell Jorge so that he could fix the headset. When she got to Jorge's laboratory, in their garage, he explained that the headset could not be repaired. A delicate wire which made it work had burned out. It was awful!

Clara went to her bedroom and stared at her fish bowl. She threw herself dramatically on the bed and started to cry. The mind-connection app was the solution, but it had failed. She felt like it was all her fault. She felt she had failed Michelle. Suddenly, someone opened the door. It was Michelle.

Clara hugged her sister and for a long time the two of them were hugging and crying. When Clara stopped crying, she thought for a moment. Michelle had come to console her. Michelle understood her. She felt it was all her fault, but realised, it was Michelle who came to give her the best loving hugs. Michelle was there when Clara needed to be comforted.

Michelle then started to flap her arms and Clara told her: 'Yes, I know you are happy. I am happy too!' Clara realised that she already knew Michelle and that Michelle knew her too. They didn't need a mind-connection app to understand each other, because they already knew each other!

It would not be easy, but they were sisters and they could stand up for each other and make things okay together. They would need to explain to the principal, to their parents, and to all the other adults. But that could be done.

They would use the Convention on the Rights of the Child

to help convince people. Anything could be done, when people were open and ready to understand each other.

Chapter 5

The alarm clock started to ring and everyone at the house woke up. The children were very excited because it was the first day of school again.

It was an even more special day because Michelle was starting at Clara's school. The school had agreed to integrate children with different abilities and Michelle was one of the first ones to join.

The sisters' dreams were beginning to come true. Michelle and Clara could go to the same school. Michelle still couldn't communicate as well as the other kids, but she could learn. The other children could learn too that each person has their own worth, and their own special gifts to bring. And together, the children could build a better future.

Welcome to Samoa!

The author of this story is Lupeoaunu'u Va'ai, or Lupe. She lives in Samoa. Lupe loves studying anything to do with the environment and experimenting with technical gadgets to see how they work. She works to support the environment in her school and her country, and she considers herself to be her family's environmental and technical expert!

One of Lupe's biggest idols is Brianna Fruean, a young environmentalist in Samoa who recently received a Commonwealth Award from the Queen for her environmental work. Perhaps Lupe's eco-warrior work will one day gain such recognition!

Lupe enjoys reading, playing the piano, playing sports, and Samoan and hip hop dancing.

THE VOICE OF AN ISLAND
Lupe Va'ai

Chapter 1

The dust was annoying, causing people to have sore eyes as well as non-stop coughing. Sitting silently in the corner of her house, Katalina thought about the beautiful stories her grandma used to tell her, of a lush, green place with colourful flowers all around. She tried to imagine the natural beauty of her land growing up, not the dry, dusty and ugly place she was now living in. Her grandma used to describe their home as if it was paradise; she talked of birds and animals in a beautiful and untouched place.

Katalina tried to imagine that same place now in her mind. It was hard. She was continuously struggling with the realities of a place that was so different from her grandma's stories – a place which was all dried up with dust all around, litter everywhere and with air so polluted one could hardly see beyond the once beautiful gardens of Vailima. Every day, as Katalina walked to school, she would see her neighbours throwing rubbish down the hills of the Alaoa Valley, families burning their rubbish in their back yards and big companies cutting down forests of trees. She felt hopeless. As a kid, she could not, in any way, tell them to stop.

It was another ordinary day: sunny, polluted and mostly dusty. When she arrived at the entrance of her school, Katalina saw the students throwing plastic bottles, twisty bags and other rubbish into the school incinerator. As she walked to her classroom, she could smell the strong smoke as it filled up the whole compound. It was like seeing her own country die before her very eyes. No one seemed to mind. No one seemed to worry. No one seemed to pay any attention to the little things that were slowly destroying her grandma's paradise.

Katalina felt as though she was trapped somewhere where she could not break free. She felt guilty that she was a part of this madness. The things her grandma had told her about were just stories, far away from the reality of the rubbish lying around and of the pollution that was surrounding her every day of her life. It did not matter how hard she tried to hang on to those memories. The truth of her life now was very real and would not disappear. She just had to live with it.

At school that day, Katalina could not focus because of the heat. The only escape was to the library and to the teachers' staff room, where there was air conditioning throughout the day. As she finished her class work for the day, she was very tired from the heat. The school water supply was being rationed due to long periods of hot weather without rain. She could smell smoke and hear the sounds of the huge trucks that were transporting logs from the Ah Li property to the Chinese factory down at the other end of the road from the school.

As she walked home, sweating from the rising temperatures of the late afternoon, she kept thinking that this must really be the end of the road for Samoa. She could feel her skin getting sunburnt. There were hardly any trees for shade along the road. She could see the other people struggling in the heat of the sun.

Arriving home, Katalina came face to face with the most shocking sight. She realised her family were part of this whole story playing out in her mind. They were also contributing to the slow destruction of her grandma's paradise.

All air conditioners in the house were on full blast. Her dad's transport business provided customers with bus services with full air-conditioning and exhaust fumes filling the air. Old vehicle parts filled up one corner of their property, which was slowly being used as a rubbish heap. She remembered overhearing one time that they were planning to dump them in Fagaloa Bay, as they were not allowed to take them to the Tafaigata landfill. Katalina thought it was also expensive for her dad to take them there.

Katalina could only think of her grandma and how she would not want her paradise to get any worse than what Katalina was already experiencing. Katalina ran outside and told her father's workers to stop all the madness. Her father was angry and asked Katalina why she made the workers stop working.

Katalina explained to him about her grandma's stories. She tried to show him what his business was doing to their quality of life. She told him about the changes to the climate in Samoa and why it was getting terribly hot and how the smoke from the buses and trucks as well as the rubbish contributed to these changes.

But her father just laughed and told her that she was a very smart girl. He called her his 'little Einstein', affectionately, but then answered that he was earning their living from doing this work. Samoa, he explained, was only a small place on earth and it would not matter what they did because the bigger countries were doing much bigger things that had a bigger impact. He also told her that the earth was made for humans to use and destroy. It was their place to do what they wanted, and Samoa was meant to be hot.

After talking to him, Katalina became very depressed and went to her room. She loved her father, but she could not believe he really understood what she was feeling and how strongly she wished for a way to restore her island to her grandma's paradise. She prayed for ideas and tried to think how to seek help. She was only a young girl and she had no idea how to reach out. She was also starting to doubt whether she was right or not and whether Samoa, like her dad said, was just meant to be used and destroyed like this.

Chapter 2

It was still boiling hot and horribly dusty the next afternoon. While walking home from school, Katalina saw cars passing her. Young children and adults were throwing rubbish out of the windows. Last week's decorations to welcome the 'All Blacks' New Zealand rugby team to Samoa were littering the roadside. Fast food wrappers were in the ditches with stray dogs going through them. The barbecue stall opposite the school was using firewood, and black smoke filled the air.

That night, Katalina could not sleep, due to all the thoughts rushing around in her young mind. She took a deep breath and closed her eyes. She kept thinking about the unfairness of growing up without being able to witness the same life and beauty that her grandma did.

Startled by the loud roar of trucks down the Cross Island road, Katalina awoke early, into yet another cloud of dust. She sighed, got ready and walked to school. She was frustrated. She knew there had to be something she could do.

Arriving at school, Katalina patiently waited in her assigned seat for the teacher. She thought of all the positive and negative impacts that people were having on Samoa, especially on her family and her village of Siumu. In Katalina's head, she was determined to save her island. She was just not sure how to go about it. She was not even sure how to bring her ideas up. They were learning about the world's Sustainable Development Goals. The teacher explained how many concerns had been recognised by the leaders of all the countries at the United Nations and how everyone had committed to stopping climate change and building a better quality of life. Katalina raised her hand. She explained about her grandma's stories and her own research. Her teacher listened and so did the class. 'It is better to try and fail than fail to try,' they said.

At break, Katalina stayed inside and started to research the things she was seeing around her. She came across some discussions on climate change and justice and the United

Nations Framework Convention on Climate Change. She also found a guide to children's environmental rights, which are protected in the United Nations Framework Convention on Climate Change and the Convention on the Rights of the Child. She understood that her concerns were shared by many, many others. She saw that promises had been made and that everyone had a role to help fulfil them.

Straight after school, Katalina raced home. The sun was beating down on her head, which felt like a pan on a wood-fired stove. But she had an idea. No matter how small it was, she was going to try it. At her house, Katalina started to list all the positive and negative impacts of the people of Samoa continuing with their current habits and lifestyles.

POSITIVE IMPACTS

- People continue to enjoy what they do
- More development in the country
- More money and resources to spend
- More fast-food, fossil fuels and fashion to use and throw away

NEGATIVE IMPACTS

- Cutting down trees will mean less clean air and the danger of landslides
- Burning and littering will keep polluting the air
- Sea level will rise and we will all have to leave Samoa
- More natural disasters in our country, fashion to use and throw away destroying our homes, and no supplies to rebuild and restore

Katalina's list kept growing, especially on the negative side. She made up her mind she was going to put her plan into action. She knew she was not going to solve the problem overnight, but felt that if she could take a little step, then it might be worth something. She picked up her camera and slipped away from her house, a clear mission in her mind. When she returned several hours later, she was both sad and inspired. She could not wait to go to school the next day, to take the next step in her plan.

Chapter 3

The next morning, Katalina woke up with her mission on her mind. Even the cloud of dust flowing unforgivingly around her house, which had become a nearly normal part of her everyday life, did not stop her from getting ready quickly and rushing off to school.

At school, she knocked on the door of her principal, Sister Masela. In order to get her message across, Katalina brought photographs of the sad situations that saw around her every day. The pictures told a thousand stories. They showed beaches covered by the waves, birds struggling in the oil and plastic floating on the tides, rubbish littering the roads, smoke pouring from factories, and children coughing in the dust. Sister Masela pledged her support for Katalina to set up the first ever 'Green Team' at St Mary's School. This became Katalina's project for the next few weeks. She was given the opportunity to speak at assembly. She explained what her new Green Team would be doing. With her teachers and friends from all school years, she set up a points system to encourage all students to learn more about the environment and to join and support her Green Team's work.

The teachers were very interested. They agreed with the principal that the Green Team points system would become part of the students' assessments, with a special award at the school's prize-giving at the end of the year. Katalina worked hard every day to write up simple things that students could do to earn points (or lose points). They could turn off electronics and taps, stop others from littering, plant a tree, walk to school, collect bottles and other materials for recycling. Her list of positive steps grew longer and longer. She even convinced her father to make small ID cards for the Green Team from cardboard materials that were already lying around at home.

After several weeks, Katalina was overwhelmed with the work and especially the interest from students. She had over 60 students who were active members and helping her with Green Team tasks and activities. Points were collected initially from the work they did in school. But slowly, the students began to do the same tasks and activities outside of school, at their homes or anywhere else they could. They were becoming part of their new habits.

The Green Team meetings were held during break time. Katalina asked her parents and teachers for help researching different environmental issues. They discussed problems like rising temperatures and sea levels, rubbish burning, deforestation, destruction of the oceans and the coral reefs, and climate change. They also discussed solutions, finding many, many ways that they could help to improve things.

Katalina realised she was not alone any more. This project became a passion for all of them. The Green Team continued to attract more members. The children continued to spread out after school to do little things in their communities that could make a difference. Some of the girls were even starting small groups in their Sunday schools and villages. Other schools began to start Green Teams too. The Green Teams each adopted a small area, at first, and began to restore it with plants, trees and flowers. Their small areas started to grow, becoming greener and cleaning the air.

Katalina could still feel the dusty air and heat in the evenings, but it did not seem to bother her as much as before. She was starting to imagine again what it looked like in her grandma's paradise. Her project to improve her surroundings had become a reality. Little by little, her Green Team was making progress. Together, they sought to bring their own island back to peace with nature – to its old self. Katalina understood that the world was changing and that Samoa had to keep up with technology, given its isolation from the rest of the world.

All the children strongly believed in their hearts that they did not have to abuse the natural surroundings and living things given by their island. Katalina thought that if she could make everyone believe this, she would have fulfilled her destiny. Word of their success spread fast. Children told their parents, their parents told their workers, their workers told their children, their children told their own schools, and so on. Katalina's Green Team collected more members each day. Even the parents wanted to join! Katalina thought that they needed as many people as possible, so she set a new target to try and have as many adults as kids.

Chapter 4

Katalina could now see the paradise in her grandma's stories slowly coming together. One by one, everything was changing from bad to good, good to great and great to brilliant.

Katalina's Green Team often arrived early at school. They shared their successes and failures from their missions over the past week. Some had good news, others not so good. More plans were made for Green Team activities. The team introduced a compost heap at school. Different bins were labelled for sorting different kinds of rubbish. Plastic bottles were placed in one and glass in another for return to the local soda company for their recycling and reuse programmes. They all felt the most important thing was the message going out. One child felt that the main town of Apia was slowly becoming aware of Katalina's Green Team. They were on a roll.

Towards the end of the year, Katalina received an unexpected surprise. It was a call to her school from the Cabinet Office, advising them that the Prime Minister of Samoa was expecting an invitation from the United Nations for a young Samoan person to make a presentation in New York on how children were implementing the Sustainable Development Goals. Invitations had been sent out to the community for nominations and somehow, Katalina's name and her work on her Green Team had come up.

She was asked if they might want to compete for the opportunity. This involved a programme in front of the government building, for all interested young people to register for a speech competition on children's commitment to saving the environment. Katalina jumped at the opportunity. This was her chance to share her concerns. It was her opportunity to communicate her ideas and work, in particular about her Green Team and what they did, and how people could support it.

To her, it was the most important chance ever – to speak

out, to let people hear her voice and importantly, spread her message on saving Samoa from the cruel impacts of climate change. She just had to help people to understand, to convince them to believe that everyone had a responsibility to help save Samoa, the Pacific Islands, and the planet Earth as well. She needed to become the voice of her island.

Katalina was very excited and could not wait for the important day to come. Many preparations were necessary. Katalina researched and studied hard so that she could learn more ways to save the environment. Her Green Team supported her with many ideas and examples for her presentation. They were determined to make sure Samoa became the paradise it once was and could once again be.

Chapter 5

The day of Katalina's presentation arrived. Like anyone, she was starting to feel nervous. Perhaps no one would listen to her. She was scared that she might make a mistake and be humiliated, and that her Green Team's work would lose credit and disappear. She was even more nervous when she arrived at the competition and saw that the Prime Minister himself was in the audience. Katalina was determined to give a good speech.

She stood up bravely. With courage, she told the story of her grandma's paradise island and how, through her young eyes, she was witnessing the loss of its natural beauty and healthy surroundings for people. Katalina talked of air pollution, the effects of rubbish not being taken care of properly, the cutting down of trees, the destruction of mangroves, and the dangers of climate change.

She spoke of the simple, everyday things that might one day make their whole island unliveable, and what could be done to change these things. She proposed all the solutions that her Green Team had tried and more.

To her amazement, the applause was thunderous. Many children approached her afterwards, to join the effort. The radio and TV interviewed her. Everyone had heard about the Green Team. She realised that they were not just applauding her words, but really, it was her actions that had convinced everyone. At the end of the competition, Katalina was selected to represent Samoa in New York. Furthermore, the Prime Minister, who was amazed by Katalina's passion, announced that Katalina had been selected as Samoa's first Child Ambassador for the Environment.

Katalina's selection as Child Ambassador was a turning point for her island. She became the face and voice for the young people, fighting for their right to a healthy environment. Many of the environmental organisations in Samoa like the Ministry of Natural Resources and Environment, Le Siosiomaga Society, Conservation International and the Secretariat of the Pacific Regional Environmental Programme asked for interviews. Katalina raced around, working hard to keep up with her Green Team's efforts, while also supporting their programmes.

In her amazing journey, Katalina had opened the minds of many people. People were more aware of their responsibilities to the environment. Everyone helped clean up the island. They banned the burning of rubbish and deforestation. Everyone thanked Katalina for her work, which had warned them of what they were doing to the country. It was not an easy task. Change was not simple and did not happen overnight. Children still walked in the dust and in the heat. But the children's voices were being heard and they were asking for something better. Many hands make light work, and islanders knew that if people come together to do simple things, it does make a change. It could save her country, Samoa, and young children like her could still make a difference. She could still experience her grandma's paradise.

Welcome to Uruguay!

The author of this story is Lautaro Real. He lives in Uruguay.

Lautaro's whole family – his parents and his little brother Lorenzo – helped with ideas for his story. At first he thought he wouldn't be able to write a story, but he is pleased with the result. He is a shy boy, except when he plays football – he loves the game and loves working in a team when he plays.

Every day Lautaro tries to help take care of the planet. He hopes one day to study engineering or architecture or to become a writer – playing football and saving the world at the same time, of course!

THE SPECIES-SAVING TIME TEAM

Lautaro Real

English translation by Odeeth Lara

Chapter 1

Once there was a boy called Lautaro who lived with many friends in a small town surrounded by rivers, low wetland forests and the sea. He grew up happy in this magical place, searching every corner for its adventures.

From the time that Lautaro was tiny, he felt different from all the children he knew. His friends always said that he was odd and very special at the same time. He dreamed of being a superhero who could save the world. He just didn't quite know how to do it!

One morning, the children were gathered in the park sharing Brazil nuts and fresh mangoes, trying to figure their friend out. His friend Paulina, who had warm brown eyes and a sharp but thoughtful voice, said, 'We are all friends, we know he is different. Lautaro always dresses strangely. He wears green trousers, shirt, and socks, and as if that was not enough, he also wears a green cape. I've seen him dressed all in green ever since I've known him. Besides, he is always surrounded by animals who follow him everywhere!'

'Also, his animals seem to have something in common,' added Camila, another friend with long black hair who loved animals and was very jolly. 'He helps and names them, and it makes them more real, somehow. His wolf dog has a green mane and a blind eye, so he gave him a patch on and named it Pirata. His jaguar with green spots is missing a part of her tail, so he's named her Media-cola. And his capybara has a floppy ear and three green stripes, her name is Rayas-verdes…'

'But the truth is that he is always kind and funny to all of us, and to animals. He is always ready to help anyone who needs him!' added Juan Pedro, who had a soft voice and a big smile. 'That is true,' said Nicolas, who was small and friendly, with joyful eyes full of play and fun, and a deep love of art and music. 'We should all be a little bit more like him. My Papa thinks that helping others makes him happy, and that's a good thing!'

'Yes, he is always very happy and funny. That is why he is our friend. We love him just the way he is,' said Santiago, who was very sporty and fast. 'My Papa says that Lautaro always asks him to help rescue some little penguin blown off course by a storm, or to help with the whales when they get caught in the shallows where our river meets the ocean. And when people gather in groups to clean the beach from the oil that sometimes washes up, Lautaro is always there.'

'My Papa also says that Lautaro tries to help his parents and neighbours. I think he is very active every day, and he finds the perfect adventure in everything he does,' replied Nicolas. The children agreed that even if Lautaro was a bit different, it was a good difference, and they were glad of it.

Chapter 2

At that very moment, Lautaro was sitting at the mouth of the river, where the fresh water flows into the sea. He was watching the waves shift the sands. Lautaro had realised that he did not want to be a superhero like the ones on television. He didn't believe in plastic heroes. But he knew that he had something special to give the world.

As he was watching the waves and sand, a collection of tiny spiky red crabs climbed out the water and settled into the sand, making a circle, like they were up to something. It seemed odd. Crabs planning something?

Lautaro's mother had told him that their home was part of a large and very special wetland, one of the largest crab habitats in Latin America, which was also home to many other species, such as capybaras, flamingos, white seagulls, and special newts.

She had also warned him that many of them were endangered species, likely to soon go extinct because their homes were being destroyed. She had explained that rights to a clean environment and to education about nature were rights that all children held, due to an old treaty called the UN Convention on the Rights of the Child.

Lautaro had been fascinated to learn about these old

promises. He was also very worried about this loss of biodiversity, and whenever he could, he would research more about animals and their ecosystem in the library and on the internet.

As he watched the crabs moving through the sand, and the sands moving with the waves, he suddenly said, 'Of course that's it! I want to be an endangered species rescuer and save all the threatened animals around the world! And I'll start right now at home, where there is already much work to be done. I'll be the superhero of all those species that are about to become extinct!'

He was overjoyed to have discovered his very own mission in life. But while he already had a green cape, he still needed a superhero name. After careful consideration he chose to be 'Capitan'.

Chapter 3

Every day, Capitan went to the mouth of their river, sat and looked at the crabs, and thought about what he could do to save the crabs, seagulls, capybaras and flamingos and all the other animals that needed help. Suddenly, as he watched, he realised he could understand exactly what the crabs were

saying, so quietly, he began to listen:

'We have to find a way to conserve our species and all the others, to avoid extinction,' said one crab. 'Without us, the whole balance of this wetland will be lost,' said another. 'Yes, our whole wetland will disappear along with us. We cannot allow this to happen,' agreed a third.

At that moment, Capitan announced, 'I will help you! I'm an eco-superhero. My name is Capitan and my mission is to help the species that are about to disappear.'

The crabs were nervous at first. To them, humans had big feet and made lots of noise and mess. They didn't see why a human might understand what they were saying!

'Don't be alarmed, I want to help you and together we can do it!' said Capitan.

Gradually, and through daily long talks and also quiet times together building things in the sand, they became very good friends. They exchanged lots of ideas for ways to achieve their goal.

Lautaro's wolf, jaguar, and capybara soon joined their circle, then the dragonflies and newts, then the white seagulls, penguins, flamingos and other birds. Soon, it was Capitan's Council of All Beings.

All of the species shared their ideas. Sometimes it was a bit difficult to understand what was going on because everyone spoke at the same time, but Capitan, as the leader, organised them to listen to each other carefully and to become respectful, so that everyone learned each other's point of view.

One day Capitan had a genius idea. Well, he thought it was a great idea. At first, when he told the crabs and his Council of All Beings, they said, 'It is not it is going to work! How we will do it? it is impossible!'

Capitan had understood that habitats were being lost for so many reasons that it would be impossible and far too costly to restore them all. But without rebuilding and restoring all the plants, clean water, soil and reeds, they could not give all the species back their homes. What they needed, he said, was a time machine. That way, they could travel back in time, and prevent everyone from hurting nature in the first place, he explained. It would be far simpler than clearing up all the damage after it was done.

The circle of crabs and the Council of All Beings were convinced. But a very young red crab piped up with the next question. 'How exactly can a circle of animals build a time machine?' Everyone looked at each other, wondering...

'It won't be difficult,' Capitan said, like a proper species-saving superhero. 'I have several ideas. You just need to trust me and to help me build it!'

'I'll recruit my friends,' he added. 'I will tell them all about the problems, and surely we will have their help too!'

Chapter 4

The next day the children had arranged to meet in the same place. The first to arrive were Santiago, Camila and Nicolas, and then everybody else arrived. Once everyone was there, Capitan told them all that had happened with crabs, and his Council of All Beings. He also told them about his idea.

Everyone looked was amazed, and struggled a bit to believe it, at first.

'A time machine?' Paulina asked. 'To return to the past and do what?'

'My Papa is certainly not going to let me join you in this idea...' replied Camila, letting herself fall onto the sand with a sad face.

'But we are all living in our own story. Parents don't get a say. We can do everything we want, as long as it is to help all the other beings,' replied Capitan.

'It's a super idea! It will be so much fun!' said Nicolas.

'We'll get things that we can recycle from our homes. We all must have something that we can use,' added Paulina.

'Well, in that case,' agreed Nicolas briskly, 'we must all meet tomorrow at the forest clearing, where we used to meet to play hide and seek.'

'And don't forget to bring recycling materials from your homes!' added Juan Pedro.

After that, Capitan went to talk to the crabs and the other beings. They had to come up with a plan so that once the time machine was ready, they could make the journey right away, and save all the species!

The next day, everyone was excited about the new project. After sunset, all the friends, children and animals, met secretly in the forest. Each brought recyclable materials to build the time machine.

The animals even had magical clocks, time-changing stones and other special treasures that they had hidden and protected for many years. Ideas flew among them happily, and they laughed as they matched their creation to Capitan's vision.

After many hours and much work a new moon rose and

they lay exhausted in the meadow to watch the wonder they just created together.

'Incredible!' they shouted at once.

'There is only a small detail,' said Paulina.

'What is it?' the rest wondered.

'I hope it works…'

Hmmm, yes, that was a tiny, little detail!

A green globe hovered above the friends, with an oval-shaped door through which they could see four soft and cosy chairs with seatbelts. The machine had a cheerful talking computer, which they called Issa. It controlled the ship along with the pilot. Their time machine was perfect and… it worked! The friends slipped away to rest, but Capitan stayed behind, still thinking about the next step.

All met again soon. This time all of Capitan's friendly beings were there, including the crabs, the flamingos, the capybaras, and many others.

'The first thing that we need to know is what has caused the extinction of many species and why so many others are dying out,' said Capitan.

A very intellectual crab knew the answer to that. 'From what I've read, the animals are endangered because when humans built cities and started using all the earth's resources, we lost many of our most important habitats.

'Endangered animals are in trouble because humankind continues to destroy the plants and to damage ecosystems and even the air and climate that the animals need to live. Humans also collect and sell exotic animals, and practise something they call sport hunting.'

'Did you know that there are over 16,000 endangered species in the world?' added a flamingo sitting next to Nicolas.

'That many? I never realised it was so bad...' said Pirata the maned wolf, blinking his good eye in surprise.

'Knowing that, we should go back to the year 1500, after the discovery of the Americas, and begin our mission there. The best thing we could do would be to help people to become aware of what will happen in the future if we don't protect animals, nature and the environment. We also have to convince all decision-makers to help us. We have to make them understand how important it is,' said Nicolas.

'After that, we will continue our trip and to land in the year 1600, then find important moments in the 1800s and 1900s. Then we can come back to home and see if our mission has been successful. Well... who will go with me?' said Capitan.

'Me!' said Nicolas.

'And me!' said Paulina, raising her hand.

'Although I'm a bit scared, I will go!' said Juan Pedro.

'I want to go too...' said Camila.

'And don't forget about us...' shouted the animals.

Unfortunately, they could not all fit inside the time machine. They had to decide who could go. 'We will decide the only possible way... talking, listening and understanding each other, like a team,' said Nicolas.

'We understand that not all of us will fit this time, but I have an idea. If our mission is successful, we could do other trips and keep on helping our planet in many ways,' Capitan added. 'We will be a Species-Saving Time Team!'

Everyone liked this idea and agreed.

Capitan, Camila, Paulina and Nicolas climbed inside the time machine. They were joined by four of their animal friends – the maned wolf Pirata, the jaguar Media-cola, the capybara Rayas-verdes and the intellectual crab. Together, they would be the first Time Team. They waved to all their friends. 'Let the journey begin!' announced Issa, their time machine.

Chapter 5

As the years sped backwards, the children watched with fascination. It was amazing. They had never imagined that travelling in time could be so exciting. It was a beautiful journey through the space-time continuum, peppered with

super-bright stars and possibilities of all colours. Issa, as their guide, while they were still amazed, tried to explain everything, so they could report back to their friends who had to stay behind.

Suddenly, the machine landed near to a river. The place was inhospitable; it looked like no one lived there. Issa said, 'Information processing... Location: Amazonian region, Ecuador... year: 1562.'

They climbed out into a rainforest and encountered a Huaorani tribe. They were greeted with caution at first, but with Issa's help, they figured out how to communicate with the tribe in their language. The Huaorani people lived from the hunt and the harvest, and understood the importance of the natural world.

They had fun together, making friends and sharing their

interests, beliefs, and traditions. Soon, they were able to understand each other very well. They left with joy after the chief assured them he and his people would continue to help to preserve and care for the animals, and would defend all nature with honour and respect.

The Time Team returned to the time machine and travelled to 1690. They stopped at a place called Santiago, in Chile, where they saw very strange and different people. They wore curious clothes and used carriages with horses to travel about. They had thick heavy clothing and tall hats. There were some very rich people, but many poor as well.

'I can't believe that they don't have computers, phones or cars,' said Camila.

'... and very few know how to read and write,' added Paulina.

As before, Issa helped them learn the way people spoke, and the children started discussing the future. They learned about the way the people lived. They also explained to them that many animal species would disappear if the people didn't care for them and understand that nature is amazing.

At first, the long-ago Chileans were very surprised, but they ended up trusting the earnest, joyful children, and promised that they would try to to protect the animals and the environment.

After a lovely feast with their new friends, the children leaped into their time machine. Feeling more relaxed, they continued their journey and stopped in 1868, in a small village called San Pablo, Guelatao, in the foothills of the Sierra Madre Mountains. While they were walking through the forest, they could not believe their eyes… many trees around the forests had been cut down and very few animals had survived. They made friends with an indigenous boy, who introduced himself as Benito.

'What is happening here? Where are all the animals?' asked Nicolas.

'People have been cutting down trees a lot lately. They have used up the soil far, far too much…' Benito answered sadly.

A big curious crowd of the Zapotec people came closer to meet Capitan, Camila, Paulina and Nicolas. They had heard that the children had something very important to share, and they wanted to meet talking animals from the future.

The children began to explain the importance of protecting animals and their habitats, including trees and the rest of the ecosystem.

'These are resources that provide for us all,' added Paulina.

'What you have said makes a lot of sense and fits our beliefs. We will do our part as well!' said Benito, excited.

The crowd looked at each other, wondering. They agreed to help, and to pass on the message to other people of the region.

As the team said farewell to the kind Zapotec people and got back to the machine, Capitan wondered if the boy was Benito Juarez, the one who made history in Mexico.

Chapter 6

It was almost time to return home, so they decided to visit 2012. Capitan believed that there was a lot of work to do there. They reached their destination at Rio de Janeiro, Brazil. There was a gathering of thousands of prime ministers and presidents from many countries. They were discussing environmental problems and the importance of protecting natural habitats for all living creatures.

The children learned that, in 1992, a first Earth Summit had been held in Rio, and all the countries had agreed a Rio Declaration on Environment and Development, with 27 principles to guide sustainable development around the world, and several international treaties.

But in 2012, there were still too many challenges, so world leaders met again, to decide on the future we want, and to agree to set Sustainable Development Goals for the world.

The children and animals were a sensation at the Rio+20 conference, and worked hard to convince all the decision-makers to make bold promises for the forests, for biodiversity, to stop climate change and to restore deserts and degraded soils.

They especially focused on changing education everywhere, so that people would respect all species. With such a dynamic Species-Saving Time Team on their side, everyone was quickly convinced, especially by the talking animals who pleaded for their survival and their habitats. Everything was agreed, and they celebrated all their achievements together.

Many people thanked them, and told them it wouldn't

have been possible without their help. It was time to return home and continue their mission of convincing all people to be good towards the environment, and that would bring them closer to living in the world they had always wanted.

As the time machine stopped, a big crowd of people and animals were waiting. As Issa announced their own time, 2032, and their faithful companions, the maned wolf, the jaguar, the crab and the capybara jumped out of the green globe, they saw thousands of crabs, flamingos, penguins and other species, that had been nearly extinct before the Time Team left, had joined their Council of All Beings. The anteaters, tapirs, sloths, howler monkeys, pumas and different species of macaw and other birds were all still in existence after all.

As the Time Team arrived, they were greeted with cheers of great joy and happiness. The children and the animals became international heroes. Together, they all began to celebrate their lives, promising to work even harder to protect each other into the future. Capitan thanked everyone, especially his friends the crabs, and all the people and the animals who had helped. They agreed that every contribution, big or small, makes a difference towards the future we want.

What are Children's Rights?

We are children. Of all ages, genders and cultures. We all have rights.

Rights are things every child has. ALL children have the same rights, no matter who they are, what religion or ethnicity they are, whatever their abilities, whatever their language, wherever they live, whether they are rich or poor… we all have the same rights.

The United Nations – a very important organisation founded in 1945 – works around the world. One of the treaties of the United Nations is called the Convention on the Rights of the Child. This Convention is very important. It has 54 articles (or sections) that cover all aspects of children's lives and it explains what we should expect, and how leaders and other adults must work to make sure we can enjoy all of our rights. Almost every country in the world has agreed to these rights, and to uphold them in law. That's over 190 nations!

First and foremost we have the right to be alive! We have the right to a name and identity, a right to be included, to be safe with access to food, clothing and shelter. We have the right to play and to rest. We have the right to an opinion! We have the right to a voice through talking, writing and drawing. We can say how we want to see the world, and adults should take our views seriously.

No right is more important than any other. Our right to play and the right to freedom of expression are no more or less important than the right to be safe from violence or the right to an education.

Can you imagine what it would be like if you couldn't do these things? Imagine if you couldn't go to school, or receive education in another way. Can you think of how that might affect the rest of your life? Richer countries have a responsibility to support poorer countries to educate the children there, to ensure that everyone has opportunities.

Imagine if you weren't allowed to play, or rest, or to spend time with the people who care for you. Some children around the world are forced into work, but this is against our rights. We have the right not to do unsafe or inappropriate work, because we are children.

Children with different abilities have the same rights, but it also states in the Convention that they have the right to be treated with dignity, and to be able to be included in play and other activities that are so important. Maybe you have different abilities, or your friends do. Let's make sure that everyone is included!

There are many rights that we have, and they are a useful tool in thinking about how we would like the world to treat all children, everywhere. Particularly it is vital to think about the right children all over the world should have to a voice in decision-making that concerns all of our futures. Together children can change the world for the better.

What are Sustainable Development Goals?

The Sustainable Development Goals were decided in 2015.

They are a way to work towards the future we wish to see, for ourselves and for all children and future generations around the world. The plan is to achieve each goal by 2030, but if we work really hard, with adults' help, perhaps we can reach them sooner.

The SDGs were informed by what the United Nations Secretary-General at the time, Ban Ki-moon, said: 'We don't have plan B because there is no planet B.'

There are 17 Sustainable Development Goals, which gives us lots to focus on!

GOALS TO DO WITH MAKING LIFE BETTER FOR ALL PEOPLE

 GOAL NUMBER 1 is for No Poverty. We could end extreme poverty by 2030 if we commit to all of the Global Goals. The target is to eradicate extreme poverty for all people everywhere. This is currently measured as people living on less than $1.25 a day, which is a very, very small amount.

Nelson Mandela, president of South Africa 1994–1999, said: 'In this new century, millions of people in the world's poorest countries remain imprisoned, enslaved, and in chains. They are trapped in the prison of poverty. It is time to set them free.'

 GOAL NUMBER 2 is for No Hunger. Governments have committed to ending hunger, and to ensuring access by all people to safe, nutritious and sufficient food all year round. This is especially the case for poor people and people in vulnerable situations, including children.

Franklin D. Roosevelt, president of the USA 1933–1945, said: 'The test of our progress is not whether we add more to the abundance of those who have much; it is whether we provide enough for those who have too little.'

When children have too little food, they are not just at

risk of illness, but they probably cannot go to school, or properly concentrate if they are in school. It's important for everyone to have enough healthy food.

 GOAL NUMBER 3 is for Good Health. Everybody deserves good health. By 2030, the aim is end preventable deaths of newborn babies and children under five years of age. We also want to end epidemics of diseases such as malaria, promote mental health and well-being, and ensure that everyone, no matter who or where they are, has access to good healthcare.

What would you do if you couldn't see a doctor?

 GOAL NUMBER 4 is for Quality Education. Let's ensure that everyone has inclusive, quality education throughout their life. This is especially the case for girls, who in many countries often don't get to go to school. Over 50 million children in the world still do not have an education.

Malala Yousafzai said: 'In some parts of the world, students are going to school every day. It's their normal life. But in other parts of the world, we are starving for education... it's like a precious gift. It's like a diamond...'

Malala Yousafzai is a big champion for girls' education, and the youngest-ever Nobel Prize Laureate. Isn't that awesome? She has used her rights, and fought very hard when at times she struggled against adults to access her rights. Now she speaks out widely to let all children, especially girls, know that they can be educated and do wonderful things.

 GOAL NUMBER 5 is for Gender Equality. There are lots of places around the world where women and girls aren't treated fairly. The aim is to end all forms of discrimination against womenand girls everywhere. Girls and women are essential to building strong and better-educated communities, but are too often affected by some of the harshest aspects of poverty. One in three girls and women experience gender-based violence in their lives. This shouldn't happen at all! Girls and women shouldn't be victims; instead they should share leadership roles alongside boys and men.

 GOAL NUMBER 6 is for Clean Water and Sanitation. Many people do not have access to clean and safe drinking water, and this situation causes disease and sometimes death. Water is often contaminated with sewage or pollution, making it very dangerous to drink. But lots of people have no choice. Children also sometimes have to walk for miles to collect water, which means they cannot go to school.

Imagine not being able to attend school, because you have to walk miles to fetch water. Or imagine having access to water, but knowing that if you drink it, that it could make you very sick. Imagine not having clean toilets to use.

 GOAL NUMBER 8 is for Good Jobs and Economic Growth. This means that all people (although not young children) should have inclusive, full and productive work. If we achieve this goal, people will not be working in unsafe environments, and also child labour will no longer happen.

Lots of children around the world still have to work very hard in dangerous conditions. For example, some children are forced to make the clothes that we wear. That's not fair, and it is against our rights as children.

 GOAL NUMBER 9 is for Innovation and Infrastructure. To end extreme poverty, we need innovative ideas, and good governments who will fund global development from every part of the community to empower people out of poverty.

Children are full of ideas! Can you think of ideas to help your government to ensure that communities all over the world can come out of poverty?

GOAL NUMBER 10 is for Reduced Inequalities. This goal was set to empower all people, regardless of their age, gender, disability, race, ethnicity, religion or any other status. Everyone should have equal opportunities. It feels awful when we aren't treated equally to other people.

 GOAL NUMBER 11 is for Sustainable Cities and Communities. This goal is to ensure that everyone, everywhere, has access to safe and affordable housing. In particular consideration must be given to children who are growing up in very poor housing situations, such as slums.

Imagine if you didn't have a safe place to live. There are still a lot of children around the world living in slum environments, or even in tents in refugee camps because they have been forced out of their own countries due to war.

 GOAL NUMBER 16 is for Peace and Justice. Everybody in the world has the right to justice and the right to live in a peaceful and inclusive society. This goal aims to end exploitation and violence, and to promote the law at all levels, allowing equal access to justice for everyone.

We shouldn't ignore any of the injustices happening in this world. We can all do something to help. We can start just by talking about them, and sharing what we have learnt.

Robert F. Kennedy, a politician in the USA in the 1960s, said: 'Every time we turn our heads the other way when we see the law flouted, when we tolerate what we know to be wrong, when we close our eyes and ears to the corrupt because we are too busy or too frightened, when we fail to speak up and speak out, we strike a blow against freedom and decency and justice.'

GOALS TO DO WITH ACTION FOR THE CLIMATE AND THE SAFETY OF THE EARTH

This is the only planet we have to live on! It is very important to protect it in every way we can.

 GOAL NUMBER 7 is for Clean Energy. Everyone should have access to clean, non-polluting energy which is especially important for protecting the planet.

 GOAL NUMBER 12 is for Responsible Consumption. We should aim to halve global food waste. We should also focus on recycling whenever we can.

We can reduce the amount of waste we produce by reusing things, and recycling what we cannot use again.

Can you think of ways you could reduce the waste you produce? Do you recycle? Perhaps you could think of more things you could reuse or recycle, to help towards a better planet for future generations.

 GOAL NUMBER 13 says that we should 'Protect the Planet with Climate Action'. Urgent action is needed to combat climate change and the terrible impact this could have on people's lives. Lots of climate-related hazards and natural disasters are becoming more common – for example tsunamis, which destroy and devastate whole communities. We can help by learning about climate change and what we can do about it. We can also spread the word, and encourage others to take the steps they can to reduce the risk of this happening. A healthy planet will take care of all future generations. All of us, now and in the future, can take care of the planet. It is our duty.

Leonardo di Caprio, the American actor, said: 'Clean air and water, and a livable climate are inalienable human rights. And solving this crisis is not a question of politics. It is our moral obligation.'

GOAL NUMBER 14 is for Life Below Water. We should conserve the oceans, by preventing marine pollution. We should also protect delicate eco-systems in the oceans.

 GOAL NUMBER 15 is for Life on Land. Just as with the oceans, we must be careful to protect forests, ecosystems, biodiversity and all life on land – it's really important for human life too!

Wangari Maathi, a Kenyan politician and environmental activist, said: 'We owe it to ourselves and to the next generation to conserve the environment so that we can bequeath our children a sustainable world that benefits all.'

Protecting the Earth promotes life for all of us living on it. Improving the environment gives people the opportunity to survive and thrive in a world free of poverty.

 The final goal, **GOAL NUMBER 17**, is that we have Partnership for all of the Goals. We need to all come together and work with each other on these goals. Let's learn about the goals, share them with our friends and family, and come together to work towards making the world a really great place for ourselves and future generations.

Voices of Future Generations

The Voices of Future Generations initiative on Children's Rights and Sustainable Development works to empower children all around the world. The children involved work hard to access their rights under the UN Convention on the Rights of the Child and most importantly to make sure other kids know their rights too. It's a rapidly growing movement to make sure that all children's voices are heard.

The project helps children to advance the right to education and literacy globally through the Voices of Future Generations Children's Book Series, based on the Convention on the Rights of the Child and the Sustainable Development Goals and authored by children aged between 8 and 12, for children aged 6 and above. These stories, gathered from a global call for child authors, are imaginative, inspiring and empowering to children all over the world. The likeable characters in the stories go on problem-solving adventures, expeditions and missions aimed at fixing specific regional problems they face in relation to their rights and sustainable development.

Through the Voices of Future Generations Intergenerational Dialogue Programme, children are able to enter into effective communication with experts and global leaders who are working towards positive change in the fields of children's rights and sustainable development. Dialogue is facilitated through intergenerational events such as children's summits, learning circles and interactive mentoring events that take place in key cities around the world. These allow children to engage effectively with world leaders and exchange ideas and solutions to issues that affect current and future generations.

We hope you enjoyed reading the stories in this anthology, as we celebrate children and what they can do to create a better future for themselves and generations to come.

We hope you find it inspiring, and perhaps you could be a future child author, writing about the ideas you have about how best to tackle some of the issues the world faces.

Voices of Future Generations: www.vofg.org